KT-417-229

The Swimmer

Graham Norton

MANCHESTER
LIBRARIES (UK)

WITHDRAWN

FROM STOCK

CORONET

First published in Great Britain in 2022 by Coronet
An Imprint of Hodder & Stoughton
An Hachette UK company

1

Copyright © Graham Norton 2022

The right of Graham Norton to be identified as the
Author of the Work has been asserted by him in accordance
with the Copyright, Designs and Patents Act 1988.

All rights reserved. No part of this publication may be reproduced,
stored in a retrieval system, or transmitted, in any form or by any
means without the prior written permission of the publisher, nor be
otherwise circulated in any form of binding or cover other than
that in which it is published and without a similar condition
being imposed on the subsequent purchaser.

All characters in this publication are fictitious and any resemblance
to real persons, living or dead, is purely coincidental.

A CIP catalogue record for this title is
available from the British Library

Paperback ISBN 9781529388015
eBook ISBN 9781529388060

Typeset by Palimpsest Book Production Ltd, Falkirk, Stirlingshire

Printed and bound in Great Britain by Clays Ltd, Elcograf S.p.A.

Hodder & Stoughton policy is to use papers that are natural, renewable
and recyclable products and made from wood grown in sustainable forests.
The logging and manufacturing processes are expected to conform to the
environmental regulations of the country of origin.

Hodder & Stoughton Ltd
Carmelite House
50 Victoria Embankment
London EC4Y 0DZ

www.hodder.co.uk

Chapter One

She had bought the old farmhouse because of the small patch of grass across the road. Helen called it her sea garden. It sloped down to the rocks and the cold ocean and was surrounded by tall pine trees that looked older than the house. They provided shade in the summer and shelter during the storms of winter.

Helen was sitting on a rough bench at a small wooden table enjoying the late afternoon sun. She had carried a tray across the road from her house. A gin and bitter lemon beside a small bowl of nuts. Perfect.

It was a Sunday evening, so the road was quiet. The only sounds were the wind in the pine trees and the soft splash of the waves. Helen let the sun warm her face as she looked up. A long streak of cloud marked the distant journey of a jet plane.

'Why would I want to be anywhere else?' she thought to herself and took a sip of her drink.

She heard footsteps on the road behind her. She turned and saw a man. Helen guessed that he was in his late thirties. He was thin with a distinctive ginger beard. He swung a blue and yellow plastic bag from Lidl.

'Lovely evening!' he called to Helen. His voice sounded as if he came from Dublin. Helen wondered what he was doing in West Cork. How had he got here? There had been no sound of a car.

'Yes. Lovely,' Helen replied.

She guessed he was going around the bend of the road to the small pub. He must be meeting friends.

She took another sip of gin and sighed.

This was how Helen Beamish had imagined her retirement. Alone and content. She had been a primary school teacher for thirty-nine years. So much talking. Parents and pupils always wanting something. Now it was her time to sit and read. That's why she had fallen in love with this old house. It was small but the view of the sea was glorious. She had never married, but living in a house beside the school meant she was never alone. She was always on call. Now she could be by herself. She bit a nut angrily. She felt like such a fool.

After Helen had lived in her new house for six months, her sister Margaret had come to stay.

She was two years older than Helen. She had married Tony Cullen and moved to live in Manchester. Helen and Margaret were not close. Then her husband Tony had died. She came to visit Helen. A holiday but nothing more. She seemed so sad. But she loved Helen's new house by the sea. Helen invited her to stay longer.

That was three years ago. The house in Manchester had been sold. A moving van had arrived. It seemed Margaret and Helen lived together. Perhaps sharing her house with anyone would have been difficult, but after three years Helen could not think of a single thing about Margaret that did not annoy her. She took another sip of gin and sighed again.

She saw a figure standing on the small pebble beach further along the coast road. People called it the Pub Cove because it was across the road from the only bar for miles. It was the red-haired man from Dublin. She could see his beard and the blue and yellow bag. His skin was very pale and he was walking into the water.

'Brave man,' Helen thought. It was only the end of May. The water must be very cold. She watched the man splash under the water and then begin to swim. It was relaxing to watch his arms dipping in and out of the waves.

Helen had enjoyed this weekend. Margaret was away. She had gone to visit her daughter in London. Was it evil to hope she never returned? Maybe Helen had lived alone for too long. She wondered if Margaret's dead husband Tony Cullen had enjoyed living with her. Surely not. Margaret treated Helen like a servant. Cups and plates left all over the house. The bin never emptied. The hoover never switched on. Helen could feel herself growing tense and angry. She must think about something else.

The swimmer was very far out now. Helen had never seen someone so far from shore. He must be halfway to the small island. She never got in the water herself, even on the hottest day. Just the thought of wearing a swimsuit made her blush. What if somebody, a man, saw her clambering down the steps? She might die of shame. Looking at the red hair moving through the dark blue of the water, she was a little jealous. He looked so free.

The sun was low in the sky now. The air had a chill and Helen pulled her cardigan closer. What would she have for dinner? There was a lamb chop that she thought was still usable. Microwave some of that spicy rice. That would do. It would make a change. Margaret looked at her as if she was from outer space if Helen put down a plate without a potato of some sort. All those years in Manchester. Had she and Tony never eaten in a foreign restaurant?

Helen did not think she was a very inventive cook, but she enjoyed pasta or a mild curry. Margaret would just push the plate away. 'I'm not hungry,' she would say with a sulk. Later Helen would find her making cheese sandwiches. Margaret would look at her sister, daring her to say something. Helen was never in the mood for a fight. She drained the last of her gin.

Maybe the drink had been too strong. Her eyelids became heavy. It was a nice feeling. Why not have a little nap? Helen felt her chin drop on to her chest. She slept.

When she woke it was nearly dark. She felt cold. Standing up, she put her glass back on the tray. A fine clear night. Hopefully tomorrow would be another sunny day. She was just stepping away from the table when something caught her eye. She put down her tray and walked to the edge of the grass. Peering into the gloom of dusk, she looked across at Pub Cove.

Was that what she thought it was? Yes. Even in this light she could see the blue and yellow of the Lidl bag. She felt uneasy. Her watch told

5

her it was nearly eight o'clock. She had been asleep for nearly an hour. Where was the swimmer? Had he just left the bag? Or was he . . .?

She did not want to ask herself that question. She tried to remain calm. What should she do? Ring 999? Was that the number for the lifeboat? Calling out a lifeboat seemed a very big step. She wasn't sure if anyone was really in trouble.

Behind the trees along the road she could see the lights of the pub. Helen decided she would check there before she did anything. Leaving the tray on the table, she stumbled across the grass to the little gate and then half walked, half ran towards the pub.

Chapter Two

Pat had never wanted to be a barman. What he did want to do was unclear, but not this. It was only meant to be a short-term job, but he had already spent nearly five years hearing the slow tick-tock of the Guinness clock on the wall of the bar. He had agreed to help out when his father had died, but now his mother was gone as well, and he was still in the pub. He had asked an estate agent about selling the place, but was told it was not a good time. Besides, he must split the money with his sister in Cork and his older brother in Limerick. There would be nothing left, and at least this way he had somewhere to live and a job.

It was quiet. Pat was surprised. It was such a nice evening he thought there might be some drinkers around. Most nights nobody came in until after nine or ten o'clock. Old farmers nursing their pint until Pat kicked them out. This pub was never going to make him rich. Pat wondered how he would ever escape.

Perched on a high stool behind the bar,

he looked more like a teenager than the man in charge. His sandy hair fell down over his eyes. It was not really a hairstyle, just the hair of someone who did not want to spend money on a trip to the barber. His broad shoulders, really too wide for his slim body, filled out an old U2 T-shirt that Pat had owned since his schooldays.

The door swung open and Pat got off his bar stool, ready to greet his first customer. He was surprised to see the retired teacher from down the road come in. She was panting and there was the glow of sweat on her brow.

Helen quickly looked around the room. No sign of the swimmer. No sign of anybody. Little wonder, she thought. The smell of old mop water, plus the harsh light from the bare bulb. This place would never draw a crowd. The young barman was staring at her. She must look half mad.

'Are you alright there?' Pat asked.

'Oh, maybe it's nothing. Was there a red-haired man in here at all?'

'No. You are my first tonight.'

'Right. Now I don't know what to do.' Helen looked back at the door.

'Were you expecting someone?' Pat asked her.

'No. I saw him swimming. He went in from

the little cove. It must be nearly two hours ago and his bag is still on the shore.'

'He might have just left it.'

'Should we call out the lifeboat?' Helen looked very worried.

Pat thought about this for a moment.

'What if we check the bag first? It might just be rubbish.'

'Good idea,' Helen said. She liked this young man. Practical. Calm.

'Let me grab my torch.' Pat reached behind the till and got a large flashlight. 'Come on.'

'What about customers?'

Pat shrugged his shoulders. 'I waited for them. They can wait for me.'

The path to the cove was narrow and uneven. Helen held on to Pat's arm to steady herself as they followed the light from the torch. On the pebble-covered shore they saw the bag. It had stones on it to stop it from blowing away.

'It doesn't look like rubbish,' Pat said.

Helen stood back.

'Hold this.' Pat gave her the torch and Helen shone it on the plastic bag. The young man bent down and looked inside. Slowly he pulled out a pair of jeans and then a pale blue shirt.

Pat looked up at Helen.

'Was he wearing these?'

'I think so. Yes.' Helen's heart had begun to beat faster. She heard a soft clink. Something hitting the ground. She moved the torch and Pat leaned forward to pick up a heavy man's watch. He stood up slowly.

'This doesn't look good. I think it's time to make the call.'

'Right.' Helen could not believe this was happening. She had thought someone would tell her she was being too dramatic, that she was an old woman who worried too much. Instead it seemed she had been right all along. Now she worried that she had wasted time.

She looked out to the cold dark sea. Was it possible that the red-haired man was still alive out there?

Pat had put the clothes and watch back in the bag. 'We must head back,' he said as he took the torch and guided Helen to the path.

An hour later, she was sat in the pub telling a policeman what she remembered. That the red-haired man had passed by her garden. That later she saw him in the water. She blushed when she had to admit she had fallen asleep. It made her sound so old. The policeman acted as if this sort of thing happened all the time.

'Not to worry. He's probably on the little island out there. Feeling cold and foolish but very much alive.'

'I hope so. I just wish I had raised the alarm sooner.'

'You did the right thing. The lifeboat is out there now. You should get home to bed.'

Helen smiled and nodded, but silently thought to herself that it was barely ten o'clock. How old did he think she was? The policeman was hardly a youngster himself. Helen had noticed that past a certain age, everyone saw you as old. Even other old people. It was very strange. She found that she did it herself.

'I made you this.' Pat put a steaming glass in front of her. 'A hot toddy. I thought you might need it.'

Helen smiled. The drink smelled so good. The whiskey, with the sharpness of the lemon and the sweet honey. It was exactly what she wanted.

'Thank you so much.' She smiled at Pat, grateful that he was just being kind and not treating her like a little old lady. She took a sip.

'Good?'

'Very!' Helen warmed her hands on the glass.

She sat back and listened to the noise from the radio in the garda car parked outside.

She could hear voices. Pat had shut the bar for the night, but people had stayed to see what was going on. Not a great deal happened out here on Horse Head so nobody wanted to miss anything.

'Can I walk you home?' Pat asked when Helen had finished her drink.

'No, no. I will be fine,' Helen replied.

'I insist. It is a dark road and there are cars out there tonight.' He picked up his torch again and the two of them headed off.

The night was very still and the sky was full of stars.

'At least it's calm,' Helen said.

'Sorry?' Pat seemed distracted.

'For the search.'

'Yes. They might find him.'

'Do you really think so?'

'The truth?'

Helen nodded her head.

'No.'

They walked in silence.

When they got to the house Helen said goodnight and Pat walked away, the light from his torch bobbing in the darkness.

Helen was about to go in when she remembered the tray she had left in the little sea garden. She picked her way carefully to the wooden table and found the remains of her drink.

Out at sea she could hear the noise of a boat's engine. A fierce bright searchlight broke through the darkness. A tunnel of light across the empty sea. If the swimmer was on the island, the lifeboat would have found him by now. The searchlight was just looking for a body.

A life was over and she had been the last person to see the man alive. Helen was cold and she knew she should go to bed, but she felt she had to stay and watch the light scanning the dark waves.

Chapter Three

They didn't look like sisters. Helen had kept her trim figure, and while her hair might be grey, she still wore it in the same short bob she always had. Helen wore clothes chosen for comfort rather than style. Plain slacks, chunky knitwear, a sensible shoe.

Margaret, on the other hand, always seemed to have a fussy bow of some sort around her neck. Matching pastel twinsets, and a fine dusting of make-up, gave her the air of someone expecting to go out. Margaret was not fat but sometimes her sister Helen had used the word *solid* to describe her. Margaret often spoke about diets but never seemed to go on one. Her hair was dyed a severe shade of black and kept in a tight perm. Helen thought it made her sister look older.

Margaret was not in a good mood. She had returned that morning ready to tell her sister all about her trip to London. Her daughter's new flat, the night at the theatre in the West End, seeing Jeremy Irons on the plane. Instead,

Helen was full of her own drama. Some young man drowning.

'Have they found the body?'

'Not yet, no.'

'So are they sure he is still out there?'

Helen knew that Margaret would be very happy if this turned out to be nothing. Helen stared at her sister. 'Well, of course we all hope he is alive, but we fear the worst.'

'We?' Margaret raised an eyebrow.

How did this woman make Helen so angry, so quickly? Helen took a deep breath to stay calm.

'The police, myself, Pat . . .' She waved her arm. She wanted Margaret to think the list was endless.

'Pat? Who is Pat?'

'Pat Carr. The young lad from the pub. He was very kind last night.'

Margaret just sniffed. Helen wanted to slap her. Instead she left the room.

Bantry was the nearest town for shopping. It was about a thirty-minute drive from the coast. Helen liked her trips to the shops. It felt good to nod to people she knew. Lorraine from the library, Barry the butcher, the woman with no name from the supermarket. A smile and perhaps a word about the weather. It made Helen feel like she was still a part of the world. It was only after she stopped teaching that she had noticed how few friends she had. As headmistress of the school, so much of her social life was meetings with parents, or fundraising for good causes.

When she moved to her new house on Horse Head, it was a shock. The house was so quiet, the days so long. Maybe that was why she had invited Margaret? If only she had waited. Now she dreamed of a long quiet day. As she walked around the supermarket, she picked up Margaret's favourite tea, the biscuits she liked, the bread she wanted for toast. It was if Helen was a guest in Margaret's house, not the other way around.

It was another sunny day and Helen enjoyed the drive home. The way the sea spread before her always lifted her spirits. She even forgot about Margaret. About half a mile from home, she was forced to pull over. A large van was coming down the narrow road towards her. It was going very fast. As it passed her, Helen saw the familiar logo for RTE News painted on the side of the van. How exciting! It must have been doing a report about the swimmer. Maybe they had found the body? Helen drove a little faster.

*

At the house, Margaret was lying on the sofa. She was exhausted. Helen did not know why. Nobody got jet lag flying in from London.

'Oh Helen, you missed all the excitement.'

'I saw the news van. Have they found anything? Do they know who he is?'

'I don't think so.'

'Right.' Helen turned to go back to the kitchen to unpack the shopping. She knew Margaret was staying on the sofa.

'I met your Pat,' Margaret said in an offhand way.

'Why?' she asked quickly, too quickly.

'He was here with the news people. They were looking for you.'

Helen hated herself for being upset, but she was. It might have been exciting to be on TV. She smiled to show Margaret that she did not care.

'Oh well, never mind.'

'Indeed.' Margaret said without looking at her sister.

After dinner, the two women sat watching television. Margaret seemed distracted.

'That was a lovely meal, Helen.'

'Thank you.' Helen sounded uncertain. Why was her sister being kind? She looked around the room. Had Margaret broken something?

The familiar music of the news played on the television.

Helen sat up.

'Oh maybe we will see the house on the news. Did they say if it was for tonight?'

'Not that I remember.'

The newsreader reported on stories from Dublin. Some scandal with taxes. A bad car crash in Galway. Then she said, 'Late yesterday a swimmer went missing off the coast in West Cork. David Egan has the latest.'

The image cut to a young man with a moustache. He was standing with a view of Pub Cove behind him. Was he in Helen's sea garden? She must ask Margaret when the report was over.

'The swimmer, a young man, has still not been named. He was last seen on the cove behind me yesterday evening. I spoke to an eyewitness, local resident, Mrs Margaret Cullen.'

And then there she was. Her tight perm steady in the sea breeze. Her red lips informing the nation of what she had seen.

'At around eight p.m., we noticed he had not returned, so we raised the alarm.' A thin smile, to show the world that she had done the right thing. The report was over.

Helen just stared at the television with her mouth open. What to say? It sounded so petty to complain, but this was not right. It was her story. This had nothing to do with Margaret. Nothing. She felt her hands shaking.

Margaret turned to her sister. She looked sheepish.

'The thing is, I—'

'Good night Margaret.' Helen stood. She was afraid she might cry. 'I am going to bed.'

She left the room and stamped up the stairs.

Chapter Four

It was silly. It was nothing. Helen was an adult and this all felt like two teenage girls sulking. About what? A man, but a man they did not know, a drowned man. Margaret had been on television. So what? Helen was not hungry for fame. Let Margaret make a fool of herself. Helen was above all of this. She knew this was true. Why then did she want to grab a wooden hanger from the wardrobe and beat her sister black and blue?

She stood in her bedroom and took deep breaths. She was not going to show Margaret that she was upset. She smiled and opened her bedroom door. Downstairs she could hear noise. Strange. When she got to the kitchen, she found Margaret standing by the cooker wearing an apron.

'Morning!' Margaret greeted her sister. 'I thought it might be nice to have a cooked breakfast for a change.'

Helen could not believe what she was seeing. Margaret had not cooked a single meal in this house.

'Lovely. Thank you.' She sat at the table.

'Eggs? Fried or scrambled?' Margaret looked happy and confident.

'Scrambled please.'

'There is orange juice in that jug.'

'Thank you.'

Helen wondered if this was about last night or had Margaret done something else. Oh well, for now she was getting a cooked breakfast. A real treat.

The meal over, Helen was just boiling the kettle for more tea when the doorbell rang.

'Are you expecting a parcel, Margaret?'

'Not me. No.' She showed no sign of getting up from the table.

'I'll get it,' Helen said, drying her hands on a tea towel.

At the door she found the policeman from the pub. He took off his cap when he saw her.

'Mrs Beamish.'

'Miss.'

'Sorry.'

'Not at all. Is there news?'

'You might say that.' The policeman paused. 'Is it okay if I come in?'

'Of course.'

Helen showed her visitor into the small sitting room at the front of the house. Her sister's voice came from the kitchen. 'Who is it?'

'It's for me,' Helen called back, loudly and firmly. She went into the sitting room and closed the door behind her.

'Sit down. Please.'

The policeman sat on the sofa. Helen chose her usual chair by the fireplace. She waited for him to speak but he was silent.

'Have you found a body?' she asked.

'No. Not yet. The lifeboat is out there again today.'

'I see.' She wanted to offer tea but did not want to go to the kitchen and risk Margaret joining her and the policeman.

'Last night we had a report of a missing person.'

Helen leaned in. 'Yes.'

'A man from Cork city. We found his car in the village.'

'The village? That is still a long walk to here.'

The policeman looked at the floor and then at Helen. 'I have a photograph. Can you have a look?'

'Of course.'

The policeman took a plastic folder out of his jacket, and then gave a photo to Helen. She looked at it. A couple at a wedding. Not the

22

bride and groom, just guests. The woman had blond hair and was holding her shoes in her hand. The man had his arm around her. He was tall and had red hair and a beard.

'Is it the man from Sunday evening?'

'I'm not sure. I think so.' In her memory the man seemed a little younger, maybe not so tall.

'Take your time.'

Helen wondered how many men with a red beard were in the area on Sunday. It must be him. The picture in her mind was wrong.

'Yes,' she said. 'That is the man I saw.'

She handed back the photograph.

'Thank you very much.' The policeman stood. 'If we have any more questions, we'll be in touch.'

'What about the watch? Is it his?'

'The wife said it is, but of course it might have been stolen.'

Helen showed the policeman to the front door. 'What happens now?' she asked.

'We keep looking. It's hard to close a case with no body.'

'I understand.'

The policeman took out his card and gave it to Helen. 'In case you think of something else.'

'Thank you.' Helen looked at the card. Detective Brian Walsh.

'Well, goodbye Detective Walsh.'

'Brian, please.' He smiled and Helen was struck by what a change it made to his face. She watched him walk to his car, and then drive away. She was not eager to face Margaret and her questions.

The following day felt like the true start of summer. Not just blue skies, but also a real heat in the sun. Helen spent the whole afternoon sitting in the sea garden reading her book.

At about five o'clock she noticed a group of people standing on Pub Cove. One was clearly a priest. He was wearing his full robes and the light sea breeze moved them from side to side. Beside him were three or four people. Helen spotted a tall blond-haired woman. Was she the person in the photograph, Helen wondered. The other people had now begun to take photographs. It was very strange.

The priest was talking. Helen was just able to hear the echo of his deep voice. Then the blond-haired woman moved to the edge of the water. She was throwing white flowers, maybe roses, into the sea. The photographers gathered around. Helen did not like the look of it all. There might be a priest, but it felt pagan. The crowd began to shuffle away towards the narrow lane to the road. Helen went back to her book.

About twenty minutes later, she heard a voice behind her.

'Hello!'

She turned. It was Pat from the pub. He was not alone. Beside him at the gate was the woman from the cove. Helen put down her book and stood.

'Pat. How are you? Lovely day.'

'It is. It is. I have someone here who wants to meet you.'

'Oh. Come in please.'

They came through the gate and walked over to Helen.

The woman took off her large sunglasses. Clearly, she had been crying. She held out her hand. 'My name is Orla. I was Tom Shine's wife.'

Helen shook her hand. It was both light and damp.

'Helen. Helen Beamish.'

Pat spoke. 'I was telling Orla that you were the last person to see Tom.'

Orla looked at Helen, as if waiting for some message from beyond the grave.

'Well, yes, I . . .' Helen did not know what to say. 'We just said hello.' Should she add that he seemed friendly? No. That was too much. He had said hello and no more. 'Will you sit?'

'Just for a moment,' Orla said and they both joined Helen at the wooden table. She noticed the other woman's large diamond earrings. Were they real? They looked it. Expensive, and her necklace didn't look cheap.

'Will I get some drinks from the bar?' Pat asked.

'No thank you,' Orla replied.

'Do you know the area well?' Helen asked.

'A little. We live in Cork.' Her eyes filled with tears. 'I live in Cork, but we came down a lot in the summer to stay with our good friend Luke.'

'Do you know him?' Pat asked Helen.

'Do I?' she asked in return.

'Tall, dark hair, has a farm just over the hill. Drives an old jeep.'

'No, I don't think so.' Helen shook her head.

A silence fell and the trio listened to the soft lapping of the waves. Helen turned to Orla.

'And have you no hope left?'

'No.' Orla looked out to sea. 'We might find a body but Tom . . .' she paused, 'Tom is gone.' A single tear rolled down her cheek. Helen marvelled that Orla was able to cry and still look beautiful.

'I should go.' Orla stood. 'Nice to meet you. Thank you for trying to help.' She gave Helen a small smile and walked away. Pat held back beside Helen.

She shook her head sadly. 'Tragic,' she said softly.

'Yes,' Pat agreed.

'Have they children?'

'No. Thank God.'

'Had they been married long?'

'I'm not sure. Childhood sweethearts.'

'Really?' Helen was confused. 'But the man, Tom, he was from Dublin?'

'No. A Cork man. They both grew up in Douglas.'

Helen frowned. Another trick of her mind.

'I better get back to the pub. A nice day. I might sell a few pints.'

Pat walked to the gate and then turned back. 'Will you come down for a drink yourself?'

Helen smiled. 'You know what? I will.' There was something about all this death that made her want to live a little.

Chapter Five

The summer drifted by. More cars on the road. The sound of children splashing in the sea. Then slowly there were more grey skies than blue, and autumn turned to winter. The road was silent once more. The light from the pub the only sign of life on Horse Head.

No body was found. A court decided that Tom Shine was dead. Death by misadventure was the verdict. Helen still worried that she might find the body. Margaret told her not to be silly. There would be nothing left by now. That made Helen feel even worse.

Pat from the pub gave Helen all the news. Orla Shine had been back. Helen wondered if she was still looking for Tom. Pat thought Orla was more interested in her dark-haired friend Luke.

'They were in here one night,' Pat said from behind the bar. 'She did not seem like a very sad widow to me.'

'Oh Pat. He is a friend. He is just comforting her.' Helen remembered Orla's tears in the sea garden.

Pat shook his head. 'Maybe you are right.'

Most Monday and Thursday nights Helen went to the pub. Pat had asked her if she played chess. She did. After dinner, she left Margaret and walked with her torch to the pub. Pat set up the board on the bar and they played chess. If a customer wanted a drink, it gave Helen more time to plan her next move. They were an even match. They both won as often as they lost. It was a little thing, but Helen enjoyed it. The winter seemed easier. Not seeing Margaret for a few hours also helped. Things were much better in the house.

It was a few weeks before Christmas. Helen had been in Bantry to shop. She was heading home when she recalled that Margaret had asked for a newspaper. She decided to stop in the village shop. Helen very rarely went in. Old Mrs Carthy who ran the shop was too much. Helen did not mind a chat, but this was more like being stopped by the police. So many questions. Helen braced herself and entered the shop. There was no sign of Mrs Carthy. Good. She bent down to pick up a newspaper. Suddenly there was a woman's voice very close to her ear.

'Was it your sister that saw the man who drowned?'

Helen jumped with surprise.

'Sorry. I did not want to startle you.'

'It's fine. Fine,' Helen said. 'No, in fact I was the one who saw him. And you were the one who found his car. Is that right?'

'Well, I saw it in the end. I felt awful. It must have been there on the Sunday, but I never spotted it until Monday night.'

'I am sure it made no difference,' Helen said. 'I fell asleep in the sun. Maybe he was crying for help.' She wasn't sure why she had shared this with old Mrs Carthy. It felt good to confess her guilt.

Mrs Carthy leaned closer. 'God forgive me, but I think that lad wanted to drown. The water off Pub Cove is very safe. He swam so far out, he did not plan on coming back.'

Helen looked around, in case anyone was listening. 'I have thought the very same thing myself.'

'And have you heard the news?'

'No. What news?' Helen asked.

'About the wife's *friend*.' Mrs Carthy said the word 'friend' as if she thought he was much more.

'Luke, you mean?'

'That's him. Well, he is selling the farm. The house, the land, the lot.'

'Why?'

'Well, I think he wants a fresh start. Maybe *they* want a fresh start.'

In the pub Pat was laughing.

'I told you! I said it was more than comfort.'

'We know nothing yet.' Helen wanted to think the best about people. 'Anyway, we all grieve in a different way. She's a widow. She is allowed to find new happiness. I wish my sister Margaret would do the same.'

Pat's face was a mixture of confusion and disgust. It seemed he was finding it hard to think about Margaret in a romantic setting. He cleared his throat as if trying to expel the very thought of it.

'Your man, Luke, better not be in a hurry to run away.'

'Why do you say that?' Helen asked.

'Selling that farm will not be easy. Half of it is rock.'

'Someone might want the house. A holiday home?'

'Well I haven't been inside it, but it looks like a ruin, and no view. It's in a dip. Great shelter but nothing else.'

'Well if he is running away with Orla—'

'He is!' Pat broke in.

'If he is,' Helen smiled, 'he won't need money.'

'No?'

'I think Orla has money. Did you notice her earrings?'

'Might be fakes?'

'Maybe, but I think not. Everything about Orla, her clothes, her hair, it all looked like money to me.'

'I bow to the woman,' Pat said. 'You know best.'

'I do, I do indeed.' She picked up a chess piece and a big smile appeared on her face.

'Checkmate!'

Christmas came and went. Margaret had gone to her other daughter in Manchester. Helen had been invited, but she politely said no. A few days without her sister was the Christmas gift she wanted. She thought she might invite Pat for dinner. But then, he told her he was going to Cork for Christmas. His aunt and uncle hosted lunch every year. Helen did not want to admit it, but the news made her sad. She had bought a chess travel set to give Pat for Christmas. Helen hid it at the back of her wardrobe. She felt foolish.

*

After the holiday was over and Margaret was back, Helen decided to skip a few chess nights in the pub. Nothing was wrong exactly, but she knew that she was too attached to Pat. She looked forward to her nights with him too much. She needed a break to allow her foolish heart to cool down.

Without meaning to, she had become . . . what? Attracted to Pat? Surely not. She did not want a romantic affair. Of course not. The very idea was absurd. No. She just liked Pat. She enjoyed his company. Helen was nearly seventy-two. How old was he? Not thirty yet.

At the same time, why not be friends? She enjoyed her nights in the pub. Where was the harm? He was at work, so she was not stopping him from going out. If he wanted to, he could easily find a girlfriend. She was not used to having a friend, especially a young man. It had confused her, that was all. She was a grown woman and she knew how to keep her feelings under control.

One morning a heavy envelope arrived for Helen. Inside was an invitation. It was for a gala dinner in Dublin the next month. Normally Helen would just say no, but this was special. It was the Irish Teachers Awards and Helen had never been. Her friend Fiona Lyons was to be given a lifetime award and wanted Helen to be there. She looked at the invitation. *Helen Beamish plus guest.* Her first idea was to bring Pat. No. That was mad. She gave a heavy sigh. She knew who her *plus one* must be.

Margaret was delighted to say yes. At once it was as if she was the one getting an award. A new dress. Calling the hotel to ask about their room.

'Twin beds please. Will there be fruit in the room? A hairdryer? An iron?'

Helen tried not to pay attention. She already knew that she was wearing her pale pink wool dress with a silk shawl. It was the outfit from her retirement party. Simple and elegant, but most of all comfortable. Margaret asked her if she was putting something in her hair.

'No,' Helen snapped. What was her sister planning? She feared the worst.

On the day, Helen drove them to Cork. Then they took the train to Dublin. A taxi took them to their hotel.

'Twenty-five euros!' Margaret was outraged by the cost of the taxi. Helen paid it with a big tip. She did not want people to think she was like her sister. In the hotel, she smiled at everyone, and said 'thank you' loudly and often. Her sister looked stern. Helen saw her rub her finger along a table. Was she looking for dust? How was this woman her sister? When they got to their room, Margaret barked orders at the man carrying their bags. Helen gave him a five-euro note. He laughed when Helen rolled her eyes in the direction of her sister.

Helen had to admit Margaret looked very nice for the dinner. Her dress was navy blue and shiny. Helen worried her pink wool might be too casual. Oh well, too late now. As they left their room Helen was nervous. She did not know why.

The sisters were sat next to Fiona. It was great to see her again. Stories from their time at training school together. Where was everyone now? Retired? Divorced? Dead? Helen looked at Margaret, but she was chatting to the very red man beside her. His bald head looked like a ball balanced on his shoulders. Where was his neck, Helen wondered. Margaret laughed a little too loudly. Was she flirting with the red-faced man? Oh well, as long as she was happy.

Dinner was to be served before the awards.

'I must not drink too much,' Fiona said.

Helen looked at her full wine glass. 'Do you mind if I do?'

'Of course not! I will catch up after my award.'

A long arm reached between the women. It was holding a basket of bread. Fiona took a roll, and the basket came to Helen. She looked up at the waiter. She knew him.

'Hello,' she said.

'Hello,' replied the waiter.

How did she know this young man? The short red beard. The red hair. All at once she remembered. It was the man on the road. It was the swimmer.

Helen tried to stand.

'I know you.'

The waiter looked unsettled.

'I really don't think so,' he said, looking around, as if for help.

The voice! It was a Dublin accent. Helen was certain this was the man. Fiona and Margaret were staring at her. Had she lost her mind?

'Horse Head. Last summer.' Helen tried to jog his memory.

'Excuse me, I . . .' The waiter turned to leave. Helen grabbed his arm, but he pulled it back and walked quickly away. She watched him make his way between the tables. She sat down.

'What was that about?' her friend Fiona

asked. Margaret leaned in, also keen to know.

Helen was breathless.

'That waiter. The one with the red hair. I saw him last summer. They said he drowned but that is him.'

'The man on Pub Cove?' her sister asked.

'Yes!' Helen was trying to see him across the room. He was talking to a waitress. They both looked in the direction of Helen.

'They never found a body,' she told Fiona, trying to help her understand. 'Excuse me. I must try to speak with him.' She stood.

'Helen. Sit down,' Margaret hissed, but too late, her sister was walking between the tables.

The red-haired waiter saw Helen. He moved quickly to a swing door and vanished. By now Helen had reached the waitress.

'Excuse me.'

'Yes?' the waitress said with a sweet smile.

'I wanted to have a word with your friend. The red-haired man.' She pointed at the swing door.

'I'm very sorry. He is ill. He has gone home.' Another sweet smile.

'Can you tell me his name at least?' Helen asked.

'I am very sorry. We are not permitted to tell people things like that.'

37

'Really? It is very important.'

'Sorry,' the waitress repeated. This time the smile looked a little rigid. She walked away.

Back at her table, Helen tried to tell the others about her chat with the waitress. 'Not even a name! Something is not right. That is the man I saw in the sea that night. So where is Tom Shine? Tell me that.' She looked at her sister and her friend. 'Where is Tom Shine?'

Margaret looked at Fiona and rolled her eyes. 'I think someone has had too much wine.'

Chapter Six

'Tell me again.' Detective Walsh looked tired. The bright lights of the garda station made his bald head glow. He wiped it with a tissue. Helen took a deep breath and began again.

'The man you showed me in the photograph was not the man I saw in the sea. The swimmer is alive and well. I saw him in Dublin. I spoke to him.'

The policeman nodded.

'Did you ask him where he went? Why he left his bag and watch?'

'I had no time. When he saw it was me, he ran away.'

The detective sighed.

'Mrs— sorry, Miss Beamish, the case is closed.'

'Please. I know you must think I am a silly old lady, but I saw what I saw.'

'You said you had seen the man in the photograph.'

'I know. I know. I spoke too soon. I only agreed it was Tom Shine because of his car being left in the village.'

The policeman leaned back. He did not think Helen was a silly old lady. He liked her. He wanted to help, but how?

'It just is not enough. I cannot reopen a case because you saw a waiter with red hair. I'm sorry.'

'Please. I called the hotel, but they refused to tell me anything.'

'You did what?' Detective Walsh was alarmed.

Helen kept speaking, not replying to the question. 'If you got a name, you could speak to Orla, Shine's wife. See how she reacts.'

'I don't know.' The policeman shook his head.

'And I told you about her friend Luke selling his farm? That must mean something.'

'It means he is selling his farm. Nothing more.'

'Please!' Helen said. 'Something is not right. Just one phone call. One.'

Detective Walsh tapped his hand on the desk. 'Okay. I will call the hotel.'

Helen stood. 'Thank you. Thank you so much.' She had the urge to hug Detective Walsh, but resisted it.

The policeman laughed. 'No promises. Now go home and be careful. There is some ice on the roads!'

'I will. I will. Thank you, Detective Walsh.' She left his office, wrapping her scarf around her neck.

After Helen was gone, Detective Walsh phoned the hotel in Dublin. No joy. That night there had been extra staff. It was all cash in hand. If they had names, it was likely that they were fake. A dead end. The detective was almost glad. No more work for him. At the same time, he wasn't happy. Helen Beamish was not a fool. Maybe on his way to work the next morning, he would pay a visit to Orla Shine. See how the widow was doing.

That night in Carr's Bar, Helen sat on her high stool. The chessboard was laid out. She told Pat everything.

'And you told the police?' he asked Helen.

'Yes. But the detective has little hope. The case is closed. What do you think?'

Pat nodded slowly and then spoke.

'Well, I always said that Orla Shine was not the normal widow. But then who is the waiter in Dublin? Why was he here swimming? Is there something to link him to Orla? And why was Tom's car left in the village?'

Helen took a sip of her gin. 'I have no idea. Detective Walsh is making some calls, but I feel there must be something that we can do.'

'Us?' Pat did not sound very certain.

'Yes. Look for clues. This is the scene of the crime,' Helen said, looking around the bar.

Pat decided not to offer her a second drink. 'Helen, we already found the Lidl bag. What else is there?'

Helen was silent for a moment, but then her face lit up.

'Pat. Do you still have your boat?'

'I do.' Pat wanted to know why she was asking.

'Why don't we go out to the island?'

'The little island past your house?' he asked.

'Yes!' Helen was very keen.

'But the guards have already searched the island.'

'Yes. Yes they did, but they were looking for a body!' Helen held up one finger. She seemed to think she had made a very good point. Pat was not certain that she had.

'And what will we be looking for?' he asked.

Helen paused for a moment. 'Well, I'm not sure, but we will know when we find it.'

Pat did not have an answer for that.

'So tomorrow morning then?' she asked him.

'It is so cold, Helen.' He did not like the idea of this older lady on the sea in winter.

'We have coats, hats, gloves! A cold wind never killed anybody!'

Pat was not so sure. Helen pulled out her torch and stood.

'I'll see you in the morning!' Helen opened the door. The cold wind nearly blew her over. 'Say ten o'clock?' she called back at Pat.

'Fine. I will see you then.' The door closed with a sharp bang.

The grass in the sea garden was crisp with frost the next morning.

'This is madness,' Margaret told her sister. 'What if you fall in? You will freeze to death before you drown.'

'Why would I fall in? The sea is like a mill-pond,' Helen said and her sister had to agree. The wind from last night was gone. The sky was a pale blue. The two women stood beneath the pine trees. The steam from their breath floated up. Margaret pulled her wool hat down over her ears. She was just about to ask where Pat was when there was the sound of an engine. The whine of the motor got louder. Pat sat at the back of the long low boat. It was wooden and painted green.

43

The boat pulled up along the rocks. 'Good morning ladies!' Pat called.

'Hello,' Helen said. She had to admit she did feel a little nervous now the boat had arrived.

'Is it both of you?' Pat asked. 'I only brought one blanket.'

'Oh only one!' Margaret called with a laugh. 'I have no desire to die today.'

'Don't be silly,' Helen said crossly. 'Now help me down.' She held out her arm and Margaret took it.

'Careful, Helen.'

Pat reached out and took her other arm, and then with one long step she was in the boat. She sat down as fast as she could.

'Good luck!' Margaret called and waved. The tone of the motor changed as Pat picked up speed and left the rocks, heading away to the island. Helen waved to her sister, trying to look happy and warm. As the boat moved forward, the air was very cold in her face.

'Good that there is no storm!' Pat shouted over the noise of the engine.

'Yes,' Helen said as loudly as she was able. She was holding on to her hat.

It only took a few minutes to cross to the small island. Pat slowed the boat down. Loud seagulls left the island in protest.

'Can we go around?' Helen asked.

'Around?' Pat was not sure.

'The far side of the island. That must be where he swam to.'

'Okay.' The boat moved through the sea. The morning sun made the water look like silk.

On the other side of the island, Pat stopped. He jumped on to a patch of stones and pulled the boat up out of the water. He tied a rope around a big rock.

'Come up this end,' he told Helen. Carefully she stepped along the boat. Then Pat put his hands under her arms and lifted her down. It felt good to be in his arms.

'Oh Helen, you have the moves of a dancer. Do you dance?'

'No. No,' she said, her face turning red. In fact that was a lie. When she was younger she had loved to dance. With her friend Fiona she had gone to so many dances. She had danced with boys. Boys had asked to see her again, but she had always said no. She wanted to study. There would be plenty of time for boys after she became a teacher. That is what she had told herself. It turned out that it had not been true. She smiled at Pat. It was too late for all of that.

'Right,' said Pat, 'what are we looking for?'

Helen was looking at the ground. 'Not sure.'

She took a few steps forward up to the rough grass. 'What is that smell?' she asked Pat.

'The birds,' he replied. 'This island is one big bird toilet.'

Helen laughed. 'Lovely.'

'Look at this,' Pat called out and Helen rushed over. He was pointing at the ground. There was a long thin mark in the soil.

Helen looked at it and then at Pat.

'What is it?'

He gave a short laugh. 'I don't know. Maybe where a boat was resting?'

Helen peered closer. 'From last summer? Is that possible?'

Pat shrugged. 'It's above the tideline. I don't know what damage the wind and rain might do. Not such a bad winter. Maybe?' He looked around, his hand above his eyes to shade them from the low winter sun. Suddenly he pointed into the grass. 'What's that?'

Helen gave a little cry. 'Oh, young eyes! What have you found now?'

Pat was on his hands and knees parting the grass. A short piece of orange nylon rope was tied to a heavy rock. It seemed so bright and alien Helen was shocked that it had not been the first thing they saw when they had got to the island.

'Cut.' Pat was holding up the end of the rope. 'Someone was in a hurry to get away.'

Helen looked around. She wanted to believe this was proof of something, but she knew that it was just a random bit of rope. Anyone might have left it. A day tripper having a picnic. A fisherman. Who knew?

'The wind is picking up,' Pat said, interrupting her thoughts. 'We should get back.' He began to walk to the shore and Helen followed. Dark clouds seemed to appear from nowhere.

'Pat?' She raised her voice against the wind.

'Yes?' He looked over his shoulder.

'If you were here with a boat and you didn't want to come back in to Pub Cove, where would you go?'

Pat stopped and considered her question.

'Across the bay? There is a little pier just over there.' He pointed towards the headland on the other side of the bay. 'They call it Mona. It's where they used to load the turf.'

Pat began walking again. They were nearly at the edge of the water when the rain started. Gentle at first but then heavy drops splashed against their faces.

Helen was picking her way through the rocks when one foot slid from under her. She let out a loud yell as she fell to the ground. Pat turned.

'Jesus! Helen, are you alright?' He rushed to her.

On the wet rocks Helen did a quick check. All her limbs moved. No sharp pain.

'I'm fine. No harm done.'

Pat stood over her. 'The fright you gave me!'

He bent to help her and she took his arm. As Pat began to pull Helen up, he too slipped and they both landed back on the ground.

'Sorry,' Pat said with a laugh. 'Some help I am. Are you alright?'

The weight of Pat's body was pressing against Helen. 'Yes.' She felt the warmth of Pat's breath against the side of her face. She turned her head and their eyes met. Helen froze. Pat's face came closer. She saw the different shades of brown in his eyes. His mouth was so close to hers. Her heart was beating with an alarming speed. Was this really happening. Was Pat about to . . .?

All at once Pat poked his head forward and placed a loud smack of a kiss on her forehead. Then, with a comedy groan, he lifted Helen to her feet in one quick movement.

'Let's get this lady home before she does any more damage.' He laughed and Helen managed to form her mouth into a smile.

She felt so stupid. No. She felt old and stupid.

How had she allowed herself to think, even for a moment, that this young man might think about her in that way? She wanted to get off this island. She wanted to be back at home with Margaret where she could feel like the sensible one.

Pat reached out a hand to help her back into the boat. She hoped that the heavy rain covered the tears rolling down her face.

Chapter Seven

Detective Walsh was in no rush to get into his office. It was a bright morning, and the sight of some snowdrops under the hedge as he got into the car had put him in a good mood. He was driving with no real destination in mind. Along the River Lee, then up the hill to look down over the city.

After his wife had died he thought he might move away. A transfer. A new start. A chance to make memories that did not include Doreen. Somehow time had slipped by and now he was happy to still be in the city. Memories of Doreen were no longer a heavy weight on him. They gave him roots. He could not imagine living anywhere else.

He had parked by a small line of shops. Nobody could say he was not working. He might be. Maybe he was watching one of these small shops. Stolen goods. Drugs. Once he had left his house, anywhere might be a crime scene. He was rooting around in his briefcase, looking for a KitKat he was sure he had not eaten, when his notebook fell out on to the passenger seat. He saw Helen Beamish's name and a few notes from his call to the hotel in Dublin. He started the engine. Today seemed like a good day to visit Orla Shine.

The house was larger than he had expected. Detached, it sat back from the road. There was an odd balcony perched on top of the porch. Brian wondered why you would ever choose to sit on it. Maybe if a parade was passing by. He examined the suburban street. That seemed unlikely.

The front garden was neat. Even in winter, someone was cutting the grass. He doubted that it was Orla Shine. He rang the bell and heavy chimes echoed through the house.

'Coming!' a loud yell came from the distance.

Brian waited, twisting his cap in his hands.

The door swung open.

'Yes?'

Orla Shine was dressed in a baby-blue tracksuit. Her blond hair was tied up with a pink scarf. Her face was make-up-free, and Brian noted that she looked even younger and prettier than the glamorous widow he had met a few months before.

'Detective Walsh. We met before. We spoke after your husband drowned.'

Orla smiled.

'Of course, Detective. Will you come in? It's all a bit of a mess. Sorry.'

Behind her Brian could see boxes.

'I don't want to interrupt. You look busy.'

'Packing up. I sold the house. After Tom . . .' she paused, 'well, after Tom the house seemed so big. I felt foolish all alone here.'

Brian felt uncomfortable. Was she flirting with him? Surely not.

'You are from here? From Cork? Is that correct?'

'I am.'

'Have you spent much time in Dublin?'

'Dublin? Well I have been there, but no, not really.'

'Have many friends up there?'

Orla had stopped smiling. 'Detective, what is this about?'

'I am sure it's nothing to worry about.' Brian hesitated. 'I do not want to upset you, but we have been contacted by someone who claims they saw your husband in Dublin.'

Orla's face hardened.

'How dare you come to me with this? You know very well where my husband is.'

'Of course. I am sorry to have to ask you these questions. It's just because the body was not recovered, we have to follow these things up. I hope you understand.'

Orla rolled her eyes. 'I suppose so, but you must understand that it is not nice to be called a liar.'

'Now Mrs Shine, no one is saying that. One last question. Have there been any attempts to take money from your bank?'

Orla folded her arms.

'My bank?'

'A joint account? Any odd activity?'

'As far as I know, everything is fine. Now, as you can see, I am a busy woman.'

'Of course. Thank you for your time.'

Brian put his cap back on and turned to walk back to his car. He heard the front door shut. On the road he looked back at the house. Did he see the curtains upstairs move? He was not certain. As he walked past the cars parked along the street, he noticed one that had a faded sticker. It said 'Head to Horse Head'. Detective Walsh stopped. The car looked familiar. Where had he seen it before?

On Horse Head Helen Beamish was in bed. Margaret was standing in her room.

'I told you not to go out to that island. I said

you would catch your death of cold and now look at you.'

Helen hated that Margaret had been proved right.

'I'm fine,' she said, but she did not feel it. Her throat was tight and she was burning up. She wanted to go back to sleep.

'Eat your soup,' her sister said. 'It will make you feel better.'

Helen moved her spoon slowly around the bowl. 'I'm sorry Margaret. I just want to sleep.'

'Right.' Margaret picked up the tray and marched out of the room. Helen wanted to remind her sister that it was Helen who had made the soup. Margaret had just stuck it in the microwave for three minutes. She turned her pillow to find a cool spot and tried to find sleep. Helen was so very tired but feared an afternoon of tossing and turning in bed.

Before long the sound of the tractor, a few fields away, began to fade and she felt sleep creep up on her. She loved this moment. Not really awake but not fully asleep. She thought she heard something. Was it the front door? It didn't matter. Margaret was down there. Her steady breathing became a gentle snore.

*

Margaret opened the door to find the garda from Cork. He was holding his cap. His smile dropped when he saw her. This was not the sister he was hoping to see.

'Detective Walsh,' he introduced himself. 'We've met before. Mrs Cullen, is it not?'

Margaret gave him one of her tight smiles. She was shocked that he had remembered her name.

'Yes. That is me. How may I assist you?'

Brian wondered how this cold aloof woman could be Helen's sister.

'Is Miss Beamish in?'

Margaret shook her head. 'She is not feeling well. A bad cold. Playing silly detective games with that Pat from the pub. At her age, I ask you.'

She looked at Brian, waiting for him to agree with her.

'Right.' The detective paused. 'Might she be up later?'

'No,' Margaret snapped. 'And please don't call again because I will be out. The cinema club in Bantry is showing *Roman Holiday*. I do not want you disturbing my sister. Am I clear, Detective Walsh?'

'Yes,' Brian replied quietly. He was not used to being spoken to like this.

Without saying anything more Margaret shut the door.

Brian sat in his car. Where should he go? Back to Cork? Maybe he would try the pub. See if Pat knew anything more. Brian had come down to Horse Head to speak to Luke Clancy, the farmer friend of Orla Shine who was selling his farm.

Luke had seemed very surprised when Brian had asked about Orla Shine. He told the detective that he was not her friend. He had not known Tom Shine. He was selling his farm because he was going to work with his brother-in-law who lived further north.

Brian was going to challenge Luke, but then he realised that he had never asked Orla about Luke. He only knew about their friendship because Helen Beamish had told him. Where had she heard about it? He had made his excuses to Luke and drove down to the coast hoping to find out more from Helen, but he was no wiser. He looked at his watch. It was only lunchtime. He had come this far. He might as well try the pub for some answers.

Margaret peered out the window waiting for the car to leave. What was he doing out there? Was it possible that the police were taking Helen and her story about the waiter seriously? Surely not?

As the afternoon wore on Margaret began to get a headache and her throat became sore. She cursed her sister, who was asleep upstairs. One moment she was burning up, the next her body shook with cold. She decided to lie down.

At the top of the stairs she knocked on Helen's door.

'Yes.'

Margaret stepped into the room. Her sister was still in bed, but reading a book.

'Nice to see you feeling better.'

'A little. Thank you. I might get up soon.'

Margaret put a hand to the side of her head. 'Lucky you. I feel awful. I am going back to bed.'

Helen put down her book. 'Oh no. I hope you didn't catch my bug.'

Margaret rolled her eyes. 'Of course I did. Thank you very much!' She left the door open and crossed the landing to her own room. The door shut with a bang.

Helen sighed. The only thing worse than being sick was having to cope with Margaret when she was ill. Helen got out of bed. She was feeling much better. She looked at herself in the mirror. Not too bad. She brushed her hair and put on a heavy wool cardigan. Tea. That was what she wanted. She went downstairs.

About half an hour later, it was dark outside. Helen was feeling hungry and wondering if she should cook something for her sister, when she heard a cry. It was Margaret calling her. Helen went to the foot of the stairs.

'Yes? What is it?'

'I have an awful head. Is there any paracetamol?'

Helen knew that there was not. She had taken the last of it that morning.

'Not sure. I'll check.'

She walked into the kitchen and waited for a few moments. Then she returned to the stairs.

'Sorry. I can't see any.'

Silence. This was classic Margaret. Helen had a strong urge to run up the stairs and punch her sister. Instead she heard herself saying, 'Would you like me to go into the village and get you some?'

A high thin voice replied, 'Oh yes please.'

'Fine. I won't be too long.'

'And Helen?'

'Yes.'

'Could you let Mrs Carthy in the shop know that I will not be going to the cinema club tonight?'

'Of course,' Helen called through gritted teeth.

Twenty minutes later, Mrs Carthy was informing Helen that the shop was out of paracetamol.

Helen was not sure what to do. She had no desire to go back and inform Margaret that she had failed.

Mrs Carthy looked at her watch.

'Tobins the chemist in Bantry has late opening tonight. If you go now you should make it.'

'Great. Thanks. I will try that.'

Driving for an hour in the dark was better than going home empty-handed.

The lights were still on in the chemist as Helen parked her car. A few minutes later she had the pills and was driving back out to Horse Head. She was in a better mood. The night air had cleared her head and she liked the feeling of a job well done. Margaret might complain that she had been gone for a long time, but she had found the paracetamol. She sang a silly song about a frog eating a fly. It was a song the children at school had loved.

When she got back to the house, Helen was surprised to find it in darkness. She was sure she had left the lamp in the hall on before she left. Maybe not. She parked the car and took the small paper bag from the chemist. Helen noticed there were no lights on in the pub. Maybe there was a power cut?

As she put her key in the lock she heard a noise. It sounded like the back door slamming. She pushed the front door but something was blocking it. She shoved harder and inched the door forward. Her hand felt along the wall for the light switch. The hall was flooded with light. Helen screamed. On the floor, pushed against the door, was Margaret in a pool of blood.

Chapter Eight

Helen hated hospitals. The smell. The harsh lights. The people sat on plastic chairs. The whole place had a feeling of fear. What was going to happen? Will they be alright? She had asked these questions, and the doctor said Margaret was going to make a full recovery. Helen found that hard to believe. Her sister was lying in a bed hooked up to several machines and drips. Most of her head was covered with bandages and the small part of her face that was visible was covered in a dark bruise. Helen sat holding her hand.

'You will be fine. You are going to be alright,' she whispered over and over again. She tried not to think about the night before, or all the other times she had been so angry with Margaret. She hated to recall all the times that she had wanted to hurt her sister. She had imagined punching her, hitting her, slapping her face. Helen let out a small sob. Now all she wanted was her sister to sit up and talk to her.

There was a tap on the door. Helen looked

up and Detective Walsh was peering around the door.

'How is she?' he whispered.

'They say she will be fine. A few stitches. Concussion. Nothing long-lasting.'

Brian stepped into the room and stood beside the bed. 'Sorry I was not there last night. I only got word this morning.'

Helen pointed at the other chair. 'Have a seat. Please.'

Brian sat down. Helen looked at her sister while she spoke.

'The police were very kind. It was awful. At first I thought Margaret was . . . that she was . . .' Helen bowed her head to hide her tears.

Normally Brian had a packet of paper tissues with him. Tools of the trade. He had left them in the car.

'Your sister is going to be fine,' he said quietly. He hoped his voice might calm Helen.

She wiped at her eyes with her hands. 'I know. It's kind of you to come.' She gave a weak smile.

'Actually I have some information. We can talk later if you want.'

'No. Now is fine.'

'I saw a report this morning. The lock on your back door was forced. Your sister was struck by the lamp in the hall. There were no finger-prints. I am sorry.'

Helen thought for a moment. 'What happened? Was it a break-in?'

'Well, nothing was taken. Maybe you disturbed them, but the report said your sister's handbag was just sitting on the kitchen table.'

'I did hear the back door.'

'Did you hear a car at all? See a car parked nearby?'

'No. But it was very dark when I got back and then when I found Margaret . . . well, it is all a blur.'

'Of course. Of course.'

From the bed came a small sound. They both looked at Margaret, but she was still asleep.

'Why would someone want to hurt Margaret?' Helen asked the detective.

'You have no ideas yourself?' Brian knew that Helen must have been thinking about this.

'Well, the only thing that struck me was that it was Margaret on television last year. Maybe someone thought she was the one who saw the swimmer. I have never met that Luke, Orla Shine's man friend. He might want to silence the only witness.'

Detective Walsh slapped his thigh.

63

'That is what I came to tell you yesterday!' His voice seemed very loud.

Helen glanced at her sister to make sure she was not disturbed.

'What?' she asked.

Lowering his voice, Brian continued, 'I went to see Luke Clancy yesterday. He claims that Orla Shine is no friend of his.'

'And do you believe him?'

'That is what I wanted to ask you. How do you know they are a couple?'

Helen thought for a moment.

'Mrs Carthy in the village shop said something about them. Pat from the pub, and, I am not certain, but I think Orla herself told me.'

'Luke Clancy says they are not friends, so who are we supposed to believe?'

'But Pat has seen them together!'

'Really?' Brian raised an eyebrow. It made Helen smile.

Margaret moved slightly in the bed. Helen stood. Was her sister awake? But no, Margaret lay still once more.

Detective Walsh cleared his throat. 'I had a thought.'

'Oh yes.' Helen sat down again.

'Who knew that Margaret was going to the cinema club last night?'

Helen looked confused.

'What do you mean?'

'Well, is it possible that someone came to the house thinking that you were at home alone?'

'You think I was the target?' Helen's face grew pale.

'I do not want to alarm you, but it does make sense. Margaret was meant to be out, leaving you all alone.'

'But the cinema club must have a hundred members or more. Everyone knew there was a film last night.'

'But not all of them knew that Margaret was planning to go. Who knew that?'

'I have no idea. Margaret might have told anyone.'

Brian nodded his head.

'True. She told me and I only spoke to her for two minutes!'

'Am I still in danger?'

Trying to sound calm and sure, Brian said, 'No. They will not be back. I can get the Bantry police to call tonight if you want.'

Helen thought about it for a moment. 'Yes, please.'

They smiled at each other. Brian stood. 'I better go. Call me if you think of anything.'

'I will, and thank you. Thanks for everything.'

'Not at all. Bye-bye. Oh, maybe call in to Pat in the pub. Let him to know to keep an eye on your place.'

'Good idea. I will.'

With a wave, Detective Walsh left the room.

Helen sat for a moment. The machines beeped and she could hear voices from the hallway. She thought about the night before. That feeling as she looked at Margaret on the ground. How she had sobbed as they carried Margaret away. Helen might not know what happened to the swimmer, or what Orla and Luke were up to, or her sister's attacker, but she had discovered something. She loved her sister. For now that was enough.

Chapter Nine

Margaret was on the news again. This time Helen was not jealous. They showed the old film of her sister talking about seeing Tom Shine. They gave the facts of the attack. Forced entry and the assault. The report said that she was comfortable in hospital and expected to make a full recovery. It was not really worthy of the news. Helen thought that they only showed it because they had the film already and the bay looked lovely. The sunshine almost made it seem like good news.

Helen had felt uneasy on the drive back to Horse Head. Was she in danger? When she got back to her house she felt better. The house still seemed like a safe place to her. Someone had put a piece of wood over the broken pane of glass in the back door. Helen guessed Pat had done the repair. She decided to thank him. Besides, the sea air would be good after spending the day in the hospital.

*

Pat looked shocked when she walked into the pub. He jumped from his stool.

'Helen. How are you? How is your sister? I heard the ambulance last night, but there were people in here drinking.'

'Were there? I thought about running here for help but there were no lights.'

'Are you sure? I was here. Strange.'

'Anyway, I am fine and Margaret will make a full recovery. Was it you that fixed the door?'

Pat held his hand up. 'Guilty. I found the bit of wood and it was easy. Saved you a job to do tonight. Drink?'

Helen hesitated. 'Oh why not? A quick one.'

She got on her usual stool at the bar and told Pat what had happened the night before. Then she began to repeat her conversation with the detective. Why would someone want to hurt Margaret? Or had Helen been the real target? Pat looked confused.

'Really, you think this was more than a random break-in?'

'Well, if it was a robber, they took nothing.'

'You came home. Disturbed them.'

'Margaret left her bag on the kitchen table. It was next to the back door. And why not hit me too instead of running away?'

'Maybe you have a point. Another?' He tapped Helen's glass.

'No. I must go home and get some sleep.'

'Will you be okay? You know what I mean, will you feel safe? Do you want me to sleep in the house tonight?'

'No, no. I will be fine.' She turned away. She could feel herself blushing. Just the thought of Pat asleep in a bed under her roof brought back unwanted feelings. Pat was a boy. He was just being kind. He had no desire to tap on her bedroom door in the middle of the night. She hurried out the door of the pub.

'Goodnight!' she called as it shut behind her.

Helen did not sleep well. She was so tired, but every tiny creak of the house made her sit up in bed. When she was not afraid of noises, she was thinking about Pat. He was a good friend. She imagined him in her room. Nothing sexual. He would just tuck her under the blankets. He might whisper goodnight. His hand reached out to stroke her hair. Then he was leaning down, his lips on hers. No! She was wide awake again and angry with herself. She had to think about something else.

Eventually, she fell into a restless sleep. When she woke, she could see light outside. It must be morning. She could hear the phone. It must have been the ringing that woke her. She jumped from her bed and rushed down the stairs. It might be the hospital.

'Hello. Hello.' She was breathless.

'Helen? Are you alright?' It was the voice of Detective Walsh.

Helen sat in the chair beside the small phone table.

'Sorry. I only just woke up. What can I do for you?'

'It's your red-haired waiter. They have found him.'

As the detective told Helen the story, it turned out that the waiter had not been found. He had walked into a garda station in Dublin and told them everything he knew.

Helen gasped and made small noises of excitement as Brian spoke. The waiter's story confirmed everything she had suspected. It was the waiter, not Tom Shine, who had walked past Helen. He was the one who got in the water. He had swum to the island and then got in a kayak that was waiting for him and paddled to the other side of the bay. He had never heard of Orla Shine or Tom Shine. He had not seen any news reports about a drowning. He had been paid five hundred euros. The man who had paid him had told him it was a prank. The only reason the waiter had come forward was because he had seen Margaret on the news and heard about the attack. He was worried that he might have been involved in a crime.

'It turns out you are quite the detective, Helen.'

Helen had no time for praise. There was only one question she wanted the answer to.

'The man. Who was the man who paid him?'

Brian paused to add to the drama. 'It was . . . Luke Clancy.'

'I knew it!' Helen punched the air. She felt like she had won a prize.

Chapter Ten

She could not sit still. After her phone call with the detective, she was filled with energy. She marched around the house. There was only one thing she wanted to do, but she knew she must wait. She put on the kettle. She called the hospital to check on Margaret. She had a shower.

It was no use. All she longed to do was rush down to the pub and tell Pat the news. She knew all the reasons why she should stop herself, but this was not about logic. Finally she gave in. He had helped her solve the mystery. She should tell him. It was the natural thing to do. There was no need to check her hair and lipstick in the hall mirror, but that is what she did before she left the house.

Standing outside the pub, Helen noticed that the curtains were drawn. Unusual. Maybe it had been a late night. She walked to the door and heard voices. She knocked and waited. There was silence. The voices stopped but nobody came to the door. Helen knocked again.

Nothing. This was very strange. Pat's car was parked where it normally was, with its little Horse Head sticker. Helen felt uneasy. Through a crack in the curtains, Helen saw movement. A flash of blond hair.

Her mind was racing. What if it was the person who had attacked Margaret? Were they in the pub trying to silence Pat? Helen wondered if she should go home and phone Brian Walsh. No. She could interrupt the attacker as she had before. She tried the door. It was open. Helen stepped into the gloom of the pub.

The first person she saw was Orla Shine. She was standing behind the bar. What was she doing here? Then in the far corner Helen spotted Pat. Beside him was a large suitcase and he was wearing his coat. The three of them stood still.

Pat was the first to speak.

'Helen.'

'What is going on, Pat?' Helen looked at Orla and then back at Pat. Were they together? The suitcase. Were they going away together?

'Just going on a little trip.' Pat spoke very softly. It was as if he was talking to a wild animal that he didn't want to spook.

'Are you and Orla Shine . . .?' Her voice trailed away. Tears sprang into her eyes.

She felt humiliated and stupid. She turned to get out of the pub, but in a single movement Pat crossed the room and put his hand on the door. He turned the key in the lock.

'Why did you have to come down here this morning?' He bowed his head and began to slide his belt out of the loops on his jeans.

'Pat.' It was Orla from behind the bar. 'What are you doing, Pat?'

Helen felt very afraid. She wanted to leave but suddenly Pat grabbed her arm. His grip was tight. He was hurting her. She gave a small scream.

'Pat, for God's sake. What are you playing at?' asked Orla.

'We can't leave her here, can we?'

Helen tried to pull away, but Pat was too strong.

'Pat, you are hurting me. Pat, you helped me. We were a team.' Even as Helen said the words, she knew how stupid they sounded.

Pat gave a short bark of a laugh. 'If I was helping you, it kept you busy. You would never think of me. Then you saw our red-haired friend in Dublin.'

Helen gasped as the truth dawned on her. 'The other night. Margaret. That was you!'

'Walsh told me she was going to be out. I meant to scare you off.'

'You nearly killed her.'

Orla came from behind the bar.

'Pat. This is too much. Tom was one thing, but this old woman has done no harm.'

Pat turned and hissed, 'She will ruin everything. If we leave her, she will raise the alarm. They will catch us at the airport.'

Orla ran her hands through her hair. 'Oh God. Oh God. We should have left at once like I said.'

Pat wrapped his belt around Helen's neck. She screamed Pat's name.

'No, Pat, this is crazy.' Orla pulled at his arm.

'Look, I'll put her body in the boat and dump her in the bay, just like we did with Tom. By the time she is missed, we will be long gone.' He began to tighten the belt.

'No, Pat. I am leaving. I want no part of this.' Orla ran to the bar, towards the back door.

Helen was trying to pull away, but she could feel the belt digging into her neck. She slipped and fell to her knees, but Pat still pulled the belt hard. She felt a pain in her chest. She needed air. Her Pat. Her lovely Pat. Why was he hurting her? Somewhere in the distance she heard a banging. A loud banging.

Chapter Eleven

A seagull drifted across the blue sky. The water was clear and the sun sparkled in the ripples. It was almost a year since Helen had watched the swimmer from her little sea garden. Now there were three people gathered around the wooden table. The bright sunshine made the green gin bottle look like a jewel.

Detective Walsh wasn't wearing his uniform. His brown jumper and yellow T-shirt gave him a relaxed air. More human, Helen thought to herself.

'I'm glad you both made a full recovery.'

'We nurse each other,' Margaret said with a laugh.

'I was fine. Just a bit of shock,' Helen added quickly. She did not want Brian to think of her as weak.

Margaret stared at her. 'Fine? Somebody tried to kill you. It was just lucky that Detective Walsh came to the pub when he did.'

Helen snorted. 'Luck? It wasn't luck. Brian used his skills as a detective. But yes, he did save me from a sticky end.' She raised her glass. 'To being saved, and happy endings!'

The three of them clinked their glasses.

'In fairness, it was really luck, Helen. I wasn't coming to save you.'

'No?' Helen asked.

'No. I had sent a car to bring Orla Shine in for questioning. I was driving down here to see Luke Clancy—'

'So why did you go to the pub?' Margaret interrupted.

'Well, I was just leaving the village when I passed the sign saying *Welcome to Horse Head* with the picture of a horse. Do you know it?'

'Yes,' both women said at once.

'That made me think of the sticker on the car I had seen outside Orla Shine's house. At the time I could not remember where I had seen the car before. On the road that day it came to me. It was always parked outside the pub.'

'I still say that is you being good at your job, not luck,' Helen assured him.

'Well, it all made sense. The only person who saw Orla and Luke together was Pat. A beautiful woman offered him an escape from his life in the pub, plus a large sum of life insurance.'

'Don't forget the sale of the house,' Margaret added.

'True. So you can see why his head was turned.'

Helen shook her head.

'Do you really think it was all her idea?'

'Don't you?' Brian asked.

'I hate to say it but I think it was him. The way he was in the pub that morning . . .' Helen closed her eyes. 'You have no idea. He was like a different man. He had fooled me all along. I thought I was being so clever. Really I was helping someone get away with murder.'

Detective Walsh reached out and touched Helen's arm. 'Don't be too hard on yourself.'

Margaret pushed her empty glass away. 'The problem was, Detective Walsh, my foolish sister had a crush on young Pat Carr.'

Helen slammed a hand down on the table. 'I did not!' All the love she had felt for Margaret in the hospital was gone.

'Ladies, please.' Brian raised his hands. The sisters glared at each other. Brian stared out to sea.

'You really do have a lovely spot here,' he said to change the subject.

'Thank you,' Helen said, a little calmer. 'Another gin?' she asked.

'A small one, please.'

'Margaret?'

'No thank you, Helen. I must see to our dinner. Will you stay, Detective Walsh?'

'No. Thank you very much. I'll just have this and go.'

Margaret stood. 'Very nice to see you, and thank you for all your help. I'm just going to peel a few potatoes.'

Helen stared at her sister. When had she ever peeled a spud? Still, she wasn't going to stop her.

Brian and Helen watched Margaret walk across the grass.

'And tell me this, are you sure Luke Clancy had nothing to do with it?' Helen asked.

'Yes. I think Pat knew that Clancy was putting his farm up for sale. A few mentions of his name here and there and he was a suspect, if they needed one.'

'And why not leave at once? Why wait?'

Brian let out a long sigh. 'Who knows? Money is my guess. They needed to sell the house. Wait for the insurance.'

Helen thought for a moment.

'It was a mad plan. Surely they were always going to be caught?'

Brian shook his head. 'They nearly got away with it. If you had not seen the waiter, there would have been no questions. Pat would have vanished. That would have been the end of the story. Even with the waiter, Pat and Orla should have stayed calm. All the waiter knew was that he had been well paid for taking a swim. With no body, if they had left the country that day, I think they would still be walking free.'

They sat in an easy silence. The waves lapped at the rocks. Helen took a sip of her drink.

'A confession. I did have a sort of mad crush on Pat Carr. I knew it was crazy. You must think I am a very silly old lady.'

Brian didn't look at her. He just stared out to sea. 'Not at all. A lonely heart will always find a way to fill itself.' His voice was soft, his words taken away by the light breeze.

Helen looked at the man sitting opposite her. She knew nothing about him. Was he a lonely heart? She decided that he was.

'Brian.' Her voice was steady and certain. 'You will stay for your dinner.'

He gave her a wide smile. 'Will I?'

'You will.'

'Well that's decided then,' Brian said and they touched their glasses together. The evening sun dragged their shadows across the grass.

THE READING AGENCY

About Quick Reads

> "Reading is such an important
> building block for success"
> - Jojo Moyes

Quick Reads are short books written by best-selling authors. They are perfect for regular readers and those who are still to discover the pleasure of reading.

Did you enjoy this Quick Read?
Tell us what you thought by filling in our short survey. Scan the QR code to go directly to the survey or visit
https://bit.ly/QuickReads2022

Turn over to find your next Quick Read…

A special thank you to Jojo Moyes for her generous donation and support of Quick Reads and to Here Design.

Quick Reads is part of The Reading Agency, a national charity tackling life's big challenges through the proven power of reading.

www.readingagency.org.uk
@readingagency   #QuickReads

The Reading Agency Ltd. Registered number: 3904882 (England & Wales)
Registered charity number: 1085443 (England & Wales)
Registered Office: 24 Bedford Row, London, WC1R 4EH
The Reading Agency is supported using public funding by Arts Council England.

Supported using public funding by
**ARTS COUNCIL
ENGLAND**

THE READING AGENCY

Find your next Quick Read:
the 2022 series

Available to buy in paperback or ebook and to borrow from your local library.

More from Quick Reads

For a complete list of titles and more information on
the authors and their books visit

www.readingagency.org.uk/quickreads

Continue your reading journey

The Reading Agency is here to help keep you
and your family reading:

Challenge yourself to complete six reads
by taking part in Reading Ahead
at your local library, college or workplace
readingahead.org.uk

Join Reading Groups for Everyone to find a
reading group and discover new books
readinggroups.org.uk

Celebrate reading on World Book Night
every year on 23 April
worldbooknight.org

Read with your family as part of the
Summer Reading Challenge
at your local library
summerreadingchallenge.org.uk

For more information, please visit our website:
readingagency.org.uk